Clifford's™ puppy days

SKATING WITH FRIENDS

by Sarah Fisch

Illustrated by Jim Durk

Based on the Scholastic book series
"Clifford The Big Red Dog"
by Norman Bridwell

ISBN-13: 978-0-439-90898-6

ISBN-10: 0-439-90898-1

12 11 10 9 8 7 6 5 4 3 2   7 8 9 10 11/0

Designed by Michael Massen

Printed in the U.S.A.

First printing, January 2007

SCHOLASTIC INC.

New York   Toronto   London   Auckland   Sydney
Mexico City   New Delhi   Hong Kong   Buenos Aires

It was January, the coldest
month of the whole year.

Lots of soft white snow
covered the playground.

"Perfect weather for a skating party, don't you think, Dad?" asked Emily Elizabeth.

"It sure is," Mr. Howard answered.

Skating party? Clifford thought. He had never heard of skating.

But he loved parties!

Emily Elizabeth was so excited, she wore

her skates at the dinner table.

"Emily Elizabeth wants to throw an
ice-skating party," Mr. Howard said.
"Can I, Mom? Please?" asked
Emily Elizabeth.

"Yes, you may," Mrs. Howard answered. "Invite some friends and we'll go to the skating rink in the park."

"HOORAY!" Emily Elizabeth shouted.

"What is ice-skating?" Clifford asked Mr. Sidarsky.

"People wear special shoes so they can glide over ice," explained Mr. Sidarsky.

"That sounds fun!" Clifford said.

Mr. Sidarsky laughed. "Dogs don't
ice-skate, Clifford!" he said.

"Why not?" Clifford wondered.

"They don't make ice skates for puppies,"

Mrs. Sidarsky said.

"Or for mice," sighed the littlest Sidarsky.

Daffodil laughed, too. "Skating isn't for
puppies, silly," she said.

"He can try," Norville said.

"Yeah!" Clifford agreed.

The day of the skating party finally came.

Clifford was so excited!

The park looked beautiful with its fresh coat of snow.

"Ready to skate, Jorgé?" Clifford asked.

Jorgé laughed. "Are you kidding?"

"Wow, look at that ice!" Nina said.

"Smooth as glass," said Emily Elizabeth.

"Let's get our skates on!"

Soon the children glided out onto the ice.

Nina twirled gracefully.

Shun could skate backward!

And Evan could skate quite fast.

Emily Elizabeth could even skate on one foot!

Clifford couldn't resist.

He ran toward the ice!

"Watch this!" he shouted to Jorgé.

But Clifford didn't glide, twirl, or jump.

He skidded, stumbled, and slid, and . . .

THUMP!

He fell into a heap on the hard, cold ice.

The tiny red puppy tried to get on his
feet, but the ice was so slippery!
And his paws were so cold!

Emily Elizabeth scooped him up in her arms. "Silly Clifford," she said, smiling and shaking her head. Clifford felt very embarrassed.

"Skating isn't for puppies," said

Emily Elizabeth.

She patted his head as she put him down.

"Don't be sad, Clifford," Jorgé said. "You were very brave to try something new. Now let's go play!"

Clifford was so glad Jorgé was there.

It was fun to dig holes together in the

fresh snow.

And they raced Evan!

Evan skated, while Clifford and Jorgé ran
alongside the skating rink.

As the sun began to set, Emily Elizabeth took Clifford in her arms. Holding him tight, she skated around and around the rink.

Everyone clapped and cheered for Clifford.

"I guess puppies can skate after all!"

Emily Elizabeth laughed.

Do You Remember?

Circle the right answer.

1. What did Emily Elizabeth wear to the dinner table?

   a. Her skates

   b. Swim flippers

   c. A cowboy hat

2. Where was the ice-skating rink?

   a. In the apartment building

   b. In the park

   c. At school

Which happened first?

Which happened next?

Which happened last?

Write a 1, 2, or 3 in the space after each sentence.

Clifford fell on the ice. _____

Emily Elizabeth wanted to have a skating party. _____

Clifford and Jorgé dug holes in the snow. _____

Answers:

Clifford and Jorgé dug holes in the snow. (3)

Emily Elizabeth wanted to have a skating party. (1)

Clifford fell on the ice. (2)

2. b

1. a